GHOUL HUNTERS

by J-P Chanda
illustrated by Patrick Spaziante

Ready-to-Read

Simon Spotlight

New York   London   Toronto   Sydney

Based on the TV series *Teenage Mutant Ninja Turtles*™
as seen on Fox and Cartoon Network®

SIMON SPOTLIGHT
An imprint of Simon & Schuster Children's Publishing Division
1230 Avenue of the Americas, New York, New York 10020

© 2005 Mirage Studios, Inc. *Teenage Mutant Ninja Turtles*™ is a trademark of
Mirage Studios, Inc. All rights reserved.

Manufactured in the United States of America

First Edition
2 4 6 8 10 9 7 5 3 1
Library of Congress Cataloging-in-Publication Data
Chanda, J-P.
Ghoul hunters / by J-P Chanda.—1st ed.
p. cm.—(Ready-to-read)
"Based on the TV series Teenage Mutant Ninja Turtles™ as seen on
Fox and Cartoon Network."
Summary: When a ghoul terrorizes the city and the Mayor
cancels Halloween, Michelangelo, Donatello, Leonardo, and
Raphael follow the clues to track down the culprits.
ISBN 1-4169-0075-6 (pbk.)
[1. Turtles—Fiction. 2. Heroes—Fiction. 3. Martial arts—Fiction. 4. Halloween—Fiction.]
I. Teenage Mutant Ninja Turtles (Television program : 2003-) II. Title. III. Series.
PZ7.C35968Gh 2005
[E]—dc22
2004027826

CHAPTER ONE

Two bank guards were on duty three nights before Halloween. Suddenly the air grew icy cold. The lights dimmed. In a flash the shrieking ghoul was floating above them!

"I've come to chew on your bonessss," it hissed and showed glowing fangs.

The ghoul shrieked, and the guards ran for their lives!

The next morning there was no money left in the bank's vault. There were also no pictures or videotape of the shrieking ghoul. But the police were used to this pattern. The ghoul had been haunting the city like this for weeks.

Night after night the ghoul had appeared at banks, museums, and stores. People told stories of its scary fangs, its evil-looking red eyes, and its loud shriek.

The whole city was in a panic.

Later that afternoon the mayor
held a meeting.

"The shrieking ghoul is a threat to
this city," he said. "I have no choice but
to cancel Halloween. No one is safe until
this menace is stopped."

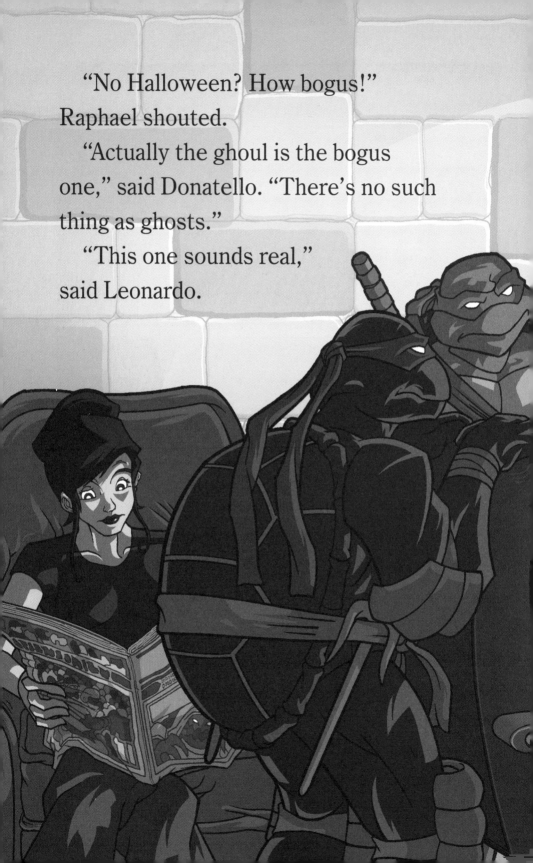

"No Halloween? How bogus!"
Raphael shouted.

"Actually the ghoul is the bogus
one," said Donatello. "There's no such
thing as ghosts."

"This one sounds real,"
said Leonardo.

"And scary," Raphael added.

"But why would a ghoul rob a bank?" April asked. "What kind of ghost needs money?"

Raphael raised his hand. "Hey, I have a question. How do you catch a ghost?"

CHAPTER TWO

The sun had set, and Michelangelo was already on the rooftops. He was sick of standing around talking about ghouls. He wanted to catch one!

Soon enough he heard a "SHRIEEEK!" a few blocks away. Michelangelo gulped and headed toward the terrible noise.

"Run! Or I'll carve you into tiny bits!" the ghoul said with a cackle. The store's security team fled.

A chill ran up Michelangelo's spine. He was feeling something very strange. He was feeling afraid!

But Michelangelo shook his head. He needed to grab the ghoul.

"COWABUNGA!" he yelled as he leaped from the shadows.

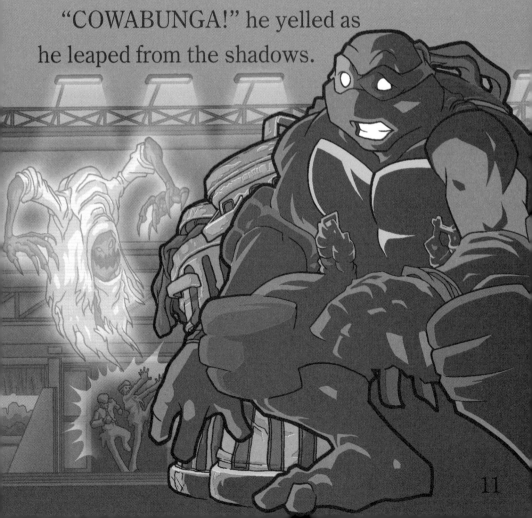

"OOF!" Michelangelo crashed to the floor. The lights had come back on, but the stock room was now empty. The ghost had vanished!

"F-f-freaky!" Michelangelo said.

Just then something caught his eye, some slimy green strands.

Back at the lair Donatello studied
the green strands. "It's seaweed," he
finally declared.

"It's our first clue," April said.

Michelangelo's voice shook as he told
them about his run-in with the ghoul.

"Sounds like you're scared, Mikey,"
Raphael said.

"Get real!" Michelangelo grumbled.
He wasn't going to admit to being scared.

"Fear is nothing to be ashamed of," Master Splinter said. "It can be a good thing. But it can also be a distraction."

"This is the perfect time to try out my latest invention," said Donatello. "Ghoul goggles—souped-up night-vision glasses that include video cameras."

Raphael gulped. "We're hunting it?"

"We have to. We can't let this thing take over the city," Leonardo said.

"Or ruin Halloween!" added Michelangelo.

CHAPTER THREE

The next night the Turtles headed to a jewelry store. They had heard a report of a ghoul-sighting there.

On the roof Donatello slid open the skylight.

Just then Michelangelo felt something breathing on his neck. He turned and saw a figure creeping toward him.

"G-g-guys!" Michelangelo called out. "It's the ghoul!"

"Ahhhh!" Raphael, Donatello, and Leonardo screamed.

But it was only Casey Jones!
"Relax, guys! I just thought you
could use some help."

"Don't sneak up on us like that!"
said Michelangelo.

"Yeah, you scared Michelangelo,"
Donatello said with a chuckle.

Michelangelo wasn't going to let
anyone make fun of him. He hooked up
his rope and jumped down into the store.

Casey and the other Turtles followed Michelangelo. The store's display cases had all been emptied!

"I don't believe a ghost did this," Donatello said.

Just then the ghoul swooped down above their heads. It shrieked as it flew further into the store.

"Grab it!" Casey shouted.

They chased the ghoul into the
back room. Then the lights went out!

The ghoul appeared in the darkness.
Its open jaw looked wide enough to
swallow them whole!

"Dead end, turtlesssss," it hissed as
green slime dripped from its fangs.

"I think I can get the lights on," Casey said. "Wait—no! Stop! Ahhhhhh!" There was a loud *thud!,* and then silence.

"Time to feast on your shellssss," the ghoul said, inching closer toward the Turtles.

CHAPTER FOUR

Just then the lights came back on. The room was empty! And the jewels weren't the only thing missing.

"Casey's gone!" Leonardo cried.

"Still think there's no ghoul?" asked Michelangelo.

"Let's look for clues," Donatello said.
The Turtles searched the whole store.
"What's that?" Michelangelo pointed
to some slime on the floor.
"Something to help us get to the
bottom of this," answered Donatello.
He scraped up some of the slime.

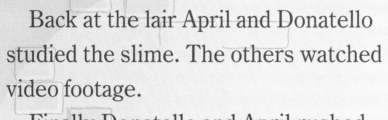

Back at the lair April and Donatello studied the slime. The others watched video footage.

Finally Donatello and April rushed in. "It's just paint!" April exclaimed. "It's glow-in-the-dark paint!"

"Meaning someone is pretending to be a ghoul," Donatello added.

"But why?" asked Michelangelo.

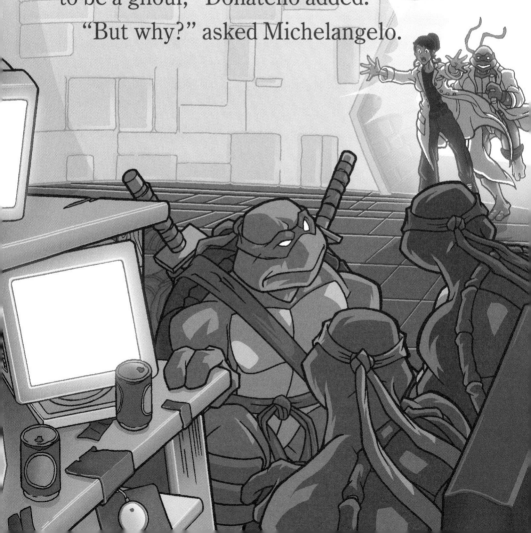

"A distraction!" Michelangelo said. "It's just like Master Splinter said: 'Fear can be a distraction.'"

Everyone looked at the tape again. This time they watched what was going on *behind* the ghoul.

"Foot Ninja!" they all said together.

CHAPTER FIVE

"Look, there's seaweed on their clothes," Michelangelo said.

"That could mean that they've been near the river," said Donatello.

The Turtles decided to take off for the docks. After almost an hour Leonardo spotted something near an abandoned warehouse.

"Bingo! Glow-in-the-dark footprints!" he said.

The Turtles followed the footprints into the warehouse. Sure enough, Casey was there.

The Turtles sneaked around the
shadows toward Casey. When they got to
him they quickly untied his arms
and pulled off his gag.

"Watch out, behind you!" Casey cried.
The Turtles turned around—and
came face-to-face with the ghoul!

"Eat this, Ghoul!" Raphael cried as he threw his sais at it. They hit a projector and—*CRASH!*—glass shattered everywhere and just like that the ghoul disappeared.

"Trick or treat!" Raphael called to the three stunned Foot Ninja who were behind the glass pieces.

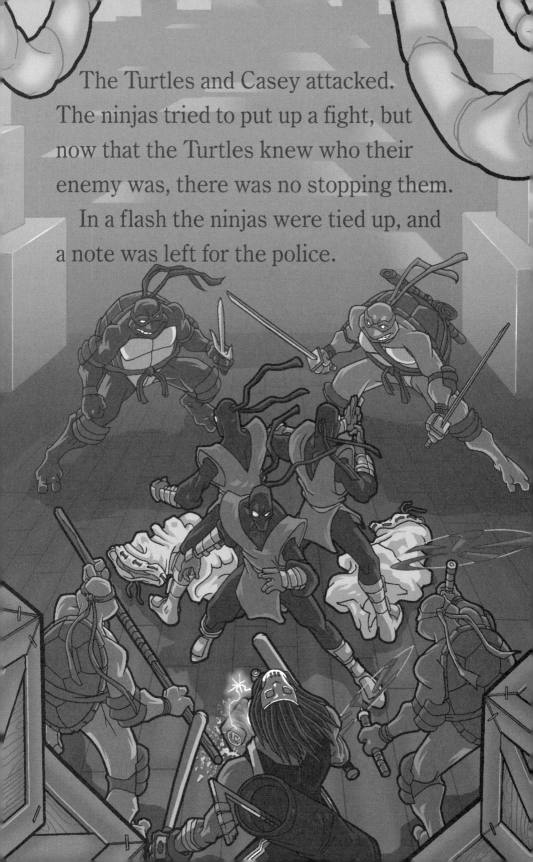

The Turtles and Casey attacked.
The ninjas tried to put up a fight, but
now that the Turtles knew who their
enemy was, there was no stopping them.
In a flash the ninjas were tied up, and
a note was left for the police.

The next day the mayor announced that the city would celebrate Halloween after all.

The Turtles couldn't have been happier. Halloween was the only night where they could walk around the streets like everyone else. Mutant turtles fit right in!

"So now do you still believe in ghosts?" Donatello asked Michelangelo, just as something tapped Donatello on the shoulder.

"Booooo!" it whispered loudly.

Donatello screamed. He took off down the street!

Casey removed his mask. "Should we tell him it was only me?"

"Not just yet," Michelangelo said.